Dream *Love*

by

Rufus Rawls

ISBN: 978-1-960853-15-8

Liberation's Publishing LLC
West Point - Mississippi

Dream Love

Rufus Rawls

Table of Content

1 Dream World 1

2 Dreamscape 7

3 Dreamtime 13

4 Dreamland 17

5 Dreamtime 23

6 Dream Vision 25

7 Dream Catcher... 37

1 Dream World

Dreams in many ways are arguably more realistic and memorable than life itself. Unlike life, you can escape a nightmarish dream by jolting yourself out of it. If it's a beautiful and gratifying dream, one that you don't want to end, the mind can relive it over and over until it becomes less and less appealing to the senses. In dreams, you go places you have never been and will likely never go. In a moment of surreal time in a fairyland, you can be transported far away to exotic or medieval places. You may encounter dangerous or adventurous life situations where you are either the victim or the hero, or the villain – the kind of person you cannot imagine yourself being. In the world of dreams, you will encounter and interact with people you have never met and may not remember having never met after you are transported from the dream world back to the bedroom. Some dreams are so beautiful and realistic that life itself is unable to match. Other dreams, however, are so unrealistic and bizarre that you cannot believe you dreamt them in the first place.

Regardless, in the world of dreams, everything

usually works out for the dreamer who sometimes imposes his or her will upon the outcome of the dream. Even so, it is oftentimes difficult to identify its source, or how the dream and the dreamer are connected. Although some dreams are prophetic, others are likely conceived from fears or desires, or they may be a way for the brain to entertain itself. Or dreams can be a way to energize the power of thought to prepare the dreamer to face life's trials and tribulations. The ability to recognize the underlying message or reason for a dream can help unravel some of life's mysteries that may otherwise remain asleep, unresolved, or buried deep within the heart that will, sooner or later, emerge unexpectedly and demand immediate attention. In any event, dreams allow the dreamers to fantasize about being the persons they are not, but really would like to be.

The narrative changes from dreams in general to the dream of a dreamer in particular: Montrose is a forty-nine-year-old male wayfarer, the main character in the unfolding of what seems to be a never-ending dream that will likely not become a reality in his life. Although he's too old to recapture his youth, he's too young at heart to give up on seeking love and happiness with the woman of his dreams. Conflicted, and now standing at the crossroads of an emotional impasse, Montrose is at odds with himself because he doesn't know which way to go.

To make matters worse, last evening before going to bed, for some unknown reason, he tried for more than an hour to remember the names of every woman he met while sowing wild oats. Not only their names, but he also tried to picture in his mind's eye the faces of each woman he wooed and courted during the romantic escapades of his heart's uncommitted love affairs. Unlike some men who complain about having had bad or even hostile relationships with women in their lives, Montrose has never had a bad relationship with any woman. He is very thankful that every woman he has ever dated was especially special and unique in distinctive ways. Each is now a fading memory, embellished to pacify his wildest dreams.

What if, he thought, my most memorable experience from each past relationship was embodied in the person of one woman? That would be, he smiled as he relished the thought, a paradise life with a paradise woman! He paused, and bits and pieces of cherished memories, smeared with uninvited regrets full of unfulfilled desires, paraded through his mind on a sentimental runway in his heart. His mind, now flooded with a barrage of yearning memories, led him to think about Darlene who was charming and sexy, always temptingly and suggestively so. Each visit to her modest but eloquently decorated apartment was an unforgettable event. She sometimes opened the door wearing an alluring negligee that revealed just enough to rouse the imagination with passionate desires leaping with expectations not so easily restrained. Or she would be eloquently dressed in an outfit perfectly suited for attending an opera or formal affair. Regardless of how she was dressed, it revealed she was keenly aware of her beauty, elegance, and sexuality.

When there was soft music playing in the background, the overall atmosphere was an enchanting prelude to an exciting evening. The dining room table was almost always decorated with candlelight and incense. When the mouthwatering smell of food filled the apartment from the kitchen to the living room, the visit was all the more enticing.

Then there was Cassandra who was breathtakingly beautiful, with a smile as refreshing as a summer breeze. Other thoughts, memories, and faces raced through his mind as if they didn't want to be recognized or remembered. But when it comes to memories, he occasionally enjoyed recalling and revisiting his past as a check and balance exercise of the mind. However, not a single memory compared with the woman of his dreams who was the kind of woman dreams are made of.

But as far as former lovers were concerned,

Montrose believed they were the source of his dreams, though the women he usually dreamed of were total strangers whom he had never met personally. His dreams were a way of imagining reliving an unlived life created from his most memorable and romantic experiences in a single relationship. Montrose's obsession with daydreaming included picturing a super life with a super-woman created from his most memorable encounters with women from his past into that of one incredible woman. It is a fantasy he embraces with hopeful expectations. Since it was unrealistic to truly believe in his fantasy, he often rethought and changed it in hopes of overcoming his doubts and fears. He also questioned himself, whether it was right for him to desire a superwoman when he was less than a superman. Unable to decide, he decided to leave the matter in the hands of fate.

He did, however, secretly confess it was a crazy idea at best. He was very thankful that only God knew what he was thinking. Nevertheless, he continued down memory lane, remembering how he and most of his friends, when they were young and foolish, lived reckless lives in the fast lane, giving little or no thought to where they were headed.

Montrose took a deep breath and fast forwarded from daydreaming to looking forward to bedtime. Each night he looked forward to returning to his dream world to spend time with the woman of his dreams who was perfect in every way. Yes! Bedtime was dreamtime in an enchanting dream world that took him to places where he met people unlike anyone or anything he had ever experienced. To be more specific, for the past six months, several nights per week, Montrose dreamed about the same woman whom he had never met but would love to have met when he was much younger. He didn't know her and didn't know if she even existed, so he affectionately christened her, Dream Love.

The weirdest thing about this particular dream, aside from it being about the same woman, is that it continued from one night to the next like the writing of an unfinished book. Whenever he dreamed about her, whether the next or several nights later, it continued from where the last episode ended. Although he didn't dream about her every night, the dream always continued in an unbroken sequence likened to that of a soap opera. In fact, the dreams caused Montrose to spend most of his daytime hours thinking about his Dream Love who filled his dream world during nighttime slumber.

2 *Dreamscape*

For a brief and delightful moment that lingered for what seemed like forever, Montrose's mind shifted again from one imaginative thought to that of paradise. Yes! His recurring ideas of paradise seemed to have been created from the most unforgettable memories and images selected from certain dreams and relationships in particular. Given most of the dreams were very fulfilling and realistic, he once again, decided to be creative and select the most exciting and meaningful memories of the women he had met during his adult life and create from those relationships or encounters one unforgettable woman. In that way, he could eliminate the unpleasant experiences, remember the beautiful and unforgettable ones, and live a life free of regrets and disappointments. At least, he convinced himself that he could create a utopian life from his dreams. Whether it was possible or not, the thought caused him to shrug his shoulders and shake his head from side to side in an attempt to make his enchanting dreams believable by mentally changing fantasies into semblances of reality.

In any event, the dreams about Dream began when Montrose had just turned forty-eight. He knew they weren't biblical, but he recalled reading in the Bible that as time nears its end, old men would dream dreams and young men would have visions. In each dream, he is either older or younger than he was in the last one, but never the same age as before. Lately, though, the most startling thing about his age in most of the recent dreams is that he was younger and not older. Sometimes, he is one to two years younger, and at other times five to six years.

Although the dreams began when he was forty-eight, he can only faintly remember his former relationships with women whom he is now convinced he never really loved, at least not the way he fantasized love to be. For one thing, he had always chosen women who chose him. He was always a gentleman to them, a suitor who still romanticizes the thought of entertaining the woman's fantasies to captivate her heart. Even so, he still yearns for that little or big something that was always noticeably missing. Although he can't quite put his finger on what was missing, it was likened to an itch he couldn't scratch. The one thing that continues to bother him the most is he can't honestly say if he has ever really loved any particular woman. However, given love is more than a feeling, but an act of the will, perhaps he had loved at least one woman along the way.

Montrose, now neither very young in his dreams nor reality, was beginning to see women in an entirely different way. During the day he sometimes took long walks in the park, and secretly watched female passersby from afar, admiring them from a mental and spiritual perspective instead of a physical one. Without stalking or appearing unmannerly, he could feel their feelings, desires, and yearnings as they walked by. The way they moved, the sparkle or the sadness in their eyes, the sound of their voices, if he were blessed to hear them talk, revealed much to him about them. It was interesting that a woman in her body was now more fascinating to Montrose than the body of the woman.

He was sometimes overcome with unfamiliar sadness when feeling the emotions of certain women as they walked by. Sadly, many of them, walking and holding hands with their man, were yearning for that missing something in their lives. Although female passersby often captivated his attention during the day, nothing took the place of his Dream Love.

So, while growing younger in his dreams, he was also becoming more thoughtful and respectful of the elderly, not that he had been disrespectful. He was not, however, thinking so much about his age or the aging process. With the benefit of hindsight, Montrose reflected on how quickly the young become old. In a sense of speaking, day–before–yesterday, the old were young, and day–after–tomorrow, they will have grown old. He exhaled and took a deep breath of welcomed relief. An odd smile cast a shadow across his face as he tried to make sense of how fast the years have come and gone. He continued to reason how the old born young are now old, and how the young are growing older day by day. He concluded the mystery of life is made manifest in the conversion of time into years, a truth Montrose clearly understood.

Although he could neither relive his youth nor postpone the passing of the years, he opted to daydream of reliving the unlived joys of yesteryears. But at the same time, he also wanted to fully embrace the gift of life each day, a gift much too precious to waste chasing mirages across the sands of time. Yes! He was daydreaming of reliving certain memories from the past as a single panoramic experience in the present. He could not, however, ignore the passing of time that happens to each of us.

Montrose was also beginning to clearly understand why his former relationships barely scratched the surface of romance and love. He had focused more on the physical side of courtship but failed to get to know the woman intimately and selflessly. Each night he looked forward to bedtime and was deeply saddened when Dream Love didn't visit him in his dreams. Since he didn't always dream about her, he was often torn between remaining wide awake and alone or going to bed and enduring a dreamless night filled with a restless presence of unfulfilled expectations. And the most fascinating thing about Dream is that she was probably a true–to–life woman whom Montrose might get to know only in his dreams, but that didn't stop him from looking forward to dreaming about her.

In any event, in the dream on this particular night, he was forty–five and was feeling like a younger version of himself. After spending the day alone on Valentine's Day, Montrose went to bed full of a nagging emptiness he had learned to live with. After finally dozing off, he was suddenly visited by an unexpected but amazing feeling that left him emotionally overwhelmed and mystified. He was forty–five in this particular dream that changed his life forever. Although he had dreamt of Dream some fifty or sixty times, they had never talked to each other.

3 Dreamtime

Surprises are unsurprising when they are expected and hoped for. A person looking forward to friends and family throwing a surprise birthday party will certainly act surprised when opening the door and everyone shouts, "Happy Birthday!" And the child, who has learned the true identity of the secret Santa, will express joy and appreciation when unwrapping gifts on Christmas morning. The most startling surprises are the ones that are unannounced, unknown, and unexpected. In Montrose's case, he looked forward to dreaming, even though they were sometimes unusual and unpredictable. He treasured the excitement of seeing how the scenes and plots developed from dream to dream, and he was never disappointed. He always looked forward to the dreams and he cherished the unexpected events that were always a source of added intrigue.

This time, Dream seemed to have appeared out of the thin air. Montrose took a deep breath interrupted by a prolonged pause in the crowded corridors of his mind. His eyes were radiant and dreamy, aglow with surprise and unexpected joy.

She looked at him and smiled. The glow on her face touched his heart in an arresting way. Montrose carefully and thoughtfully formed a word or two on the tip of his tongue but was unable to give voice to them.

Dream continued to look at him. Her smile was defined with girlish happiness and purity. Her eyes were transfixed on Montrose. Her dimples beckoned unto him to say something to break the unnerving silence.

Montrose somehow knew Dream was thirty. He felt an onset of fear and tension in his throat that was choking his voice. Unsure of what to say or how to say it, he finally mumbled nervously, "Had I met you when I was your age, we would have had a wonderful life together!"

Dream added a smile to her smile. "What about now? We met when we met! Anyway, are you saying you're too old for me?"

Montrose thought long and carefully before answering. He didn't know whether she was asking him a serious question, or just teasing and flirting with him for the fun of it.

Did she see him as a lover and father figure fittingly wrapped up in an aging man? Or was she looking for a sugar daddy, a benefactor – someone she could give her leftover affection to while looking forward to a budding and loving relationship with someone much younger? A thousand and one possibilities raced through the thoughts that were bombarding his clouded mind. He was unsure if he could trust the barrage of conflicted emotions pounding on the door of his heart. He was also unwilling to believe she was interested in him for the same reasons he was interested in her. He, to his surprise, felt like a frightened child, though he tried to hide it, trapped in the middle of a busy intersection surrounded by speeding vehicles going in and coming in and from every direction. He seemed to have been hopelessly trapped and unable to avoid being run over by an onrush of winding thoughts and emotions.

Despite feeling trapped, he still believed he could have had a wonderful life with Dream, had they met when he was her age. Although the thought was intriguing, he concluded it was probably a fairytale at best. Anyway, barely old enough to be her father, he was afraid to answer her one way or the other, but finally uttered, "No, I'm not too old for you. You're too young for me!"

Her eyes sparkled with pure delight, but she said nothing. Instead, she slowly and carefully placed her left forefinger in an upright position on her slightly moist lips. She was eloquently dressed in a slightly wrinkled, no-frills, gray jogging suit. Her presence, though a dream, radiated a joy that caused his heart to pant for her. The added intrigue, he was dreaming a dream within the dream. Tossing and turning, he was hoping to wake up from dreaming and find Dream beside him in his bedroom. While grappling with what to say, he was awakened and jolted back to the loneliness that he sometimes escaped during his serialized dreams. Instead of getting out of bed, he tossed and turned until he finally fell into a deep sleep. Within several minutes the dream continued, but with a strange twist of events that he had not experienced before…

4 *Dreamland*

Alone and lonely, in the next breathtaking moment, she appeared at his side. At first, their conversation was expressed in calm and peaceful silence. Montrose knew she was sent to fill his emptiness, and neither the need nor the desire to talk was necessary. They were the total of each other's unfulfilled selves that gave their togetherness true meaning.

The next incredible moment they were bicycling, riding without any particular sense of direction, purpose, destination, or need. They were simply enjoying riding their bikes like two excited children on Christmas morning, surrounded by the beauty of nature in its most glorious and purest majestic splendor. The soothing warmth of the radiant sunlight danced around their heads and gently rested upon their shoulders. Her freshly ironed, snow-white jeans were spotless and unblemished. Her light brown skin radiated an inexplicable and blissful presence.

Montrose and Dream rode and rode, pedaling side-by-side, ignoring everything around them, including the traffic, long enough to feast their eyes on each other. Her eyes sparkled with an angelic innocence unpolluted by the cares of life. As they pedaled with the greatest of ease, her long hair danced on the wings of the wind, enjoying the experience with the same unrestrained happiness that was aglow on her face. Montrose now trailed Dream very closely, following her every twist and turn like an inseparable shadow on the sunny afternoon that it was. His love for her was boundless, unquenchable, and unrestrained. He wanted nothing about them to ever change. He was willing to follow her wherever life took them.

Dream stopped near the underpass at Meadowbrook Road and Northbrook Drive, and talked at length with a mysterious trucker who was there waiting for her. Montrose watched them from afar. He thought it was strange to see the driver of an eighteen-wheeler dressed in a black tuxedo. Dream's hair appeared to have been outstretched in the now stilled wind. Her conversation with the trucker was punctuated with calm and friendly gestures. Given the aura and joy that Montrose and Dream's relationship personified, pure and precious as life itself, thoughts of jealousy were as absent as the wind.

Once back together, Dream calmly shared that a man she saw kill a young woman was now determined to kill her! The trucker had nothing to do with the plot. It was just her appointed time to tell Montrose about it.

Thoughts of her death seemed as unlikely as the

moon falling from the heavens in the next ten seconds. Yet the thought caused him to break out in a cold sweat. "Aren't you afraid?" he asked her with unsettled nervousness in his voice.

"Yes! I'm afraid for him," she quickly and thoughtfully replied.

Montrose loved her so very much! He dared not entertain any sexual fantasies or thoughts of even touching her in an unmannerly way unbecoming a gentleman. Her very presence blessed him with all the beauty and joy his heart desired. He was grateful for each precious moment they were sharing.

Now bicycling again, their eyes were locked on each other in a spellbinding gaze that only their hearts understood. Without warning, romantic thoughts marked "posted" were awakened in Montrose's mind and broke through the door to his heart that was holding them hostage. If saying "I do" would have joined them together as husband and wife in holy matrimony, he would have happily said, "I do" a thousand times over!

Dream somehow knew the depth of his love for her. Even the secret thoughts he tried to hide behind or within silence were common knowledge to her.

When their bikes almost collided, she reached out and grasped his left hand with a tender touch. Whenever his right pedal was up, her left pedal was down. With her hand now resting gently in the center of his back, life opened its abundant heart to them. At that moment, life could offer them nothing more.

In the next unforgettable moment, Dream disappeared, and Montrose was driving someone's car with a female passenger he didn't know. The traffic was as heavy as a thick fog. It reminded him of a traffic jam from a sellout crowd leaving a football game at Memorial Stadium. Just ahead a train was nearing the railroad crossing on Northside Drive. To his right, he saw Dream walking slowly but purposefully toward the tracks. Also, to his right and slightly behind her was a badly dented, old red Plymouth sedan swerving in and out of the traffic.

"My God, he's the man who wants to kill her."

His bloodshot eyes were transfixed on Dream. While ignoring the traffic, he raised his pistol and aimed it at her walking just ahead of his car.

"With all of these people, he's going to shoot her!" Montrose shouted and raised a pistol that somehow or the other appeared in his right hand. His decision to shoot the gunman was almost as frightening as the thought of Dream being shot by him.

Montrose aimed and squeezed the trigger. The large pistol broke the eerie silence hovering just above the noise of the traffic. He never blinked an eye.

As if blessed with supernatural eyesight, Montrose

saw the bullet curve and zoom by the gunman's head through the opened windows and out the driver's side of the red Plymouth.

Dream would escape if she could only reach the railroad crossing before the train…

Most of the cars were now gone. An ambulance parked near the tracks remained. The driver, an assistant, and three policemen stood near Dream's covered body.

With his weapon drawn and in plain sight, the gunman jumped from the red Plymouth and ran from vehicle to vehicle.

His and Montrose's eyes met each time he tried to dump the pistol. Unable to escape Montrose's policing eyes, the gunman turned and walked angrily to the ambulance, turning his back to one of the police officers that continued to talk as he handcuffed him.

"Is Dream dead?" Montrose asked. His voice was weak and trembled with fear and unbelief.

"Yes," one officer calmly stated as if he was discussing a stray animal.

Dream's serene face was partly veiled by her long hair. Montrose kneeled beside her. Praying she was only asleep; he snatched the blanket from her body!

"My God, is she dead?" He questioned the question already answered by the police officer.

Although there were no visible wounds, blood trickled from her nose and from beneath the sweatband that hugged her forehead.

The ambulance driver picked Dream up from the hot pavement, slung her across his shoulder, and walked away, leaving the ambulance behind.

Montrose looked around. Everyone had disappeared! Only the blinking lights reflecting off the ambulance proved she was not a figment of his imagination.

Dream Love was much more than a dream…

5 *Dreamtime*

He quickly sat up in bed and looked around. The only sound he heard was the erratic throbbing of his heart beating against the walls of his chest. The loud pounding reminded him of being awakened at midnight not too many evenings ago by a distressed neighbor beating frantically on his door. He dragged the back of his left hand slowly across his face and took a prolonged look into the pitch-black darkness of the night that filled the room. He, trying to remember exactly where he was, took several deep breaths to calm himself. After some thought, he wondered if Dream was symbolic of the woman he would meet or was she nothing more than the ending of an unrealistic dream to his dream of finding a true love to fill the void he was struggling to overcome.

What had been a beautiful and loving dream was now a living nightmare. Instead of looking forward to going to bed each night, Montrose tried to avoid sleep altogether. And, whenever he neared the railroad crossing at the busy intersection on Northside Drive, he saw in his mind's eye the flashing lights and heard the deafening sounds of an oncoming train, even when no train was coming. When a train was nearing the crossing, the flashing lights and the blaring horn were much more than a warning of what was coming. The train was an unforgettable reminder of what had passed, and a prophetic sign of the love that was yet to come…

6 *Dream Vision*

As the slow-moving days and the longest of nights came and went, Montrose dreaded sleep most of all because Dream no longer visited him during the night. After several months, he learned to sleep without expecting to dream about her. But on this particular midsummer morning, when he least expected anything exciting to happen, he went to the park that he and Dream often visited in his dreams and sat on a wobbly bench near the bike trail. Without expecting to see anyone or anything, in particular, he saw a beautiful woman riding her bike toward him. He tried not to look at her, but before he could yield or resist the temptation to look or not, she stopped directly in front of him. She was sporting a jogging outfit that modestly hugged her body. The gray, no-frills jogging outfit was slightly faded from wear and tear. The telltale signs revealed it had outlived its fashionable years. Even though it was no longer stylish, it looked as dazzling on her as she did in it.

Her hair was flung across the left shoulder. It was sunny and hot. Her lipstick and facial makeup were unblemished. Montrose instinctively, without planning to, compared her to Dream Love.

Before he could say anything, she asked him,

"What're you doing here today?" The question captured his attention because she stressed today with special emphasis.

"Nothing, nothing at all," was his truthful answer. She smiled and looked at him as if they were unfamiliar friends. "Do you come here often?'

"No, not really."

"Me either." She got off the bike slowly, carefully let the kickstand down with undivided attention, and sat close to Montrose in the middle of the bench. He slowly shifted his leg to avoid touching hers.

Montrose looked up at the treetops as if he expected the woodland to speak for him.

"I don't know why I came here today." She paused. Took a minute to rethink her thoughts. "It's almost like I was drawn here. Do you know what I mean?"

"Yes, sort of, I guess." Montrose spoke as if he was talking to himself in her presence. "May I ask you a question? It's kind of personal, one that most women don't like to be asked."

"What's the question?" she inquired with a curious twinkle in her eye.

"How old are you?" He asked passively and timidly with an unsettling sense of urgency, though he didn't expect her to tell him.

"I'm thirty… Today's my birthday!" She instinctively raised her arms high above her head with cheerful gestures choreographed to perfection.

"Wow, that's amazing."

"Why, why is it amazing?" she asked pointedly.

"I don't know. It just is," Montrose replied.

"And you, how old are you, and what's your name?"

"I'm forty-nine, going on a hundred." His voice descended into a melodic, humorous whisper. "My name is Montrose."

They both laughed at the same time, followed by complete silence.

"Okay," Montrose finally asked, "What's your name?"

"Jessica…Jessica Love."

Time stopped in the space they were occupying, and everything around them was caught up in that moment. Montrose wanted to stand up and run, but his entire body was paralyzed on the bench. He was convinced he was dreaming wide–awake or sleepwalking in a nightmarish trance in the heat of the day. He was left speechless and motionless for several seconds that seemed much longer. He was in a desperate struggle to escape being drawn into whatever it was that he was experiencing.

As his mind ricocheted off of cherished memories framed with a backdrop of renewed hope, his uninvited past collided with the emotions that were bombarding his mind.

Dreaming about Dream Love was one thing. Whatever it was that was now happening to him was not a dream, but perhaps an encounter birthed out of his dreams. He was struggling to go forward in his mind without returning to memories that he was determined to forget. Yet, he was remembering things he was trying to forget. Sure! He loved the idea of reliving certain experiences, while un-living any sorrowful memories attached to them. He carefully thought about what he should say to her but was afraid to say what he was thinking. His thoughts were running nonstop outside of their emotional boundaries. He tried to toss them aside by saying nothing while thinking about what to say.

Jessica broke the uncomfortable flurry of silent noise. "Why, why do you want to know my age? Do you have some kind of hang-up with a young woman like me?" She stood and spun around to emphasize like me!

Montrose, still sitting, was shifting his feet from side to side to calm himself. The plush green grass limited his erratic movement. His mind stumbled into the past and unleashed a barrage of conflicting thoughts that were closing in on him. "No, it's just that you remind me of someone I used to dream about several nights a week. The dreams stopped when she was killed in the last dream, I had of her."

Jessica tilted her head slightly to the left and ran her fingers through her hair. "Maybe she wasn't a dream." "Maybe she's not dead," she added after giving serious thought to her words.

"Anyway, it's your birthday? Why are you alone?"

Montrose quickly changed the conversation. "I'm not alone. I'm here with you right now."

A smile ran across her face. Her mind seemed to have been focused on the thought more than it was on Montrose.

"We're together right now. I'm not alone!"

"Yeah, I know, but you know what I mean?" Still standing, she walked in a small circle.

"No, I don't know. What do you mean?" The question was asked with a touch of bold innocence, followed by several hand gestures to stress its importance.

Montrose was finally able to stand. He took several steps in his mind, but his feet never moved. "What I mean is, you didn't know I'd be here today."

She shortened the borders of the circle, turning slowly within it, carefully avoiding stepping over its imaginary boundaries. "But you're here. I'm here. We're here."

Montrose was fascinated and annoyed by the way she responded to everything he said. "I can't argue with that," he mumbled in a low voice that she could barely hear.

He then opened his mouth to say something that she could hear, but once again silence ruled his tongue. Amid total silence, a single teardrop formed in the left corner of his left eye, crawled slowly down his face, and sneaked quietly into the corner of his mouth that graciously received it. His tongue was waiting patiently in the left corner of his mouth for that single tear to prevent an emotional floodgate from opening up.

Montrose hoped Jessica didn't see what he was doing, though he was much more concerned with figuring out how to handle himself at that moment. He knew very little about how the tear duct works and was both puzzled and amazed by that single teardrop. He wanted to know where it came from. Do tears know when to flow? Do they know the difference between happy and sad eyes? Was that single teardrop invited, or was it summoned by emotional feelings evoked by questions that his heart wanted answered? He didn't know the answers to his unvoiced questions that were full of perplexing intrigue. If he shared them with Jessica, she might think they were dumb and meaningless. Regardless, he needed them answered. He wanted to know how to prevent other tears from coming out of their secret hiding places.

Montrose can remember crying silently only two or three times in his entire life. It wasn't that he had always tried not to cry. It's just that he rarely did. So, during this embarrassing episode, on the verge of crying, he fought to push the tears back. Not wanting Jessica to see him cry, an emotion he was unfamiliar and uncomfortable with, he walked around the circle that she was walking in. He looked and looked and looked at her looking at him looking at her. After stuttering, muttering, and rambling for the longest in the silence of his mind, he cleared his throat and said, "Anyway, I was just thinking, had I met you when I was your age, we could've had a wonderful life together!"

He remembered saying the same thing to Dream in a dream. He felt stupid saying it to Jessica, yet he felt compelled to, like he had no choice. Plus, he wanted to see what she would say, though he didn't expect her to do or say what she said.

Although she had never experienced this before, Jessica was stricken with a severe headache that registered at least a ten on the Richter scale of pain. With eyes barely opened, she gently massaged her forehead for several seconds. A faint smile spoke a thousand words unspoken by her heart. After carefully pondering what Montrose had said, she was visited by a feeling of alluring wonder. "That's a beautiful, heartfelt thing to say to me." She paused. Although unsure of what else to say, or how to say it, she was very careful not to say the wrong thing, or the right thing the wrong way.

"Anyway, how is it possible for you to have met me when you were my age? I'm nineteen years younger than you!"

Montrose, a bit embarrassed, thought long and hard before answering her. "Yes, nineteen years younger you are for sure!"

The expression on his face changed from that of a confident man to a shy child. "I can't… It couldn't… But had I met you when I was your age…" He took a deep breath and exhaled quickly to prevent the thought from causing his heart more grief. "Still, I can only imagine."

Jessica, with sentimental caution staring her in the face, thought about thinking about Montrose's dream becoming a reality. "Sure, you and me, we could settle for only imagining, but what good is that? What about us? What about now? Forget what could have been. Think on what is; what can be."

The soothing sound of her voice came from the depths of her heart. With a sparkle in her eyes, she smiled and shrugged her shoulders, turned abruptly away, went to the bike, and placed her left foot on the right pedal. Each of her actions captivated Montrose's attention. He felt emotional shock waves flood his body.

Jessica then walked slowly away from the bike, and stopped directly in front of Montrose, breathing slowly and deeply with an irregular heartbeat. They searched for the right words to explain what their hearts were feeling.

"Well, we met when we met, didn't we? Anyway, are you saying you're too old for a thirty-year-old like me?" She stressed the question with graceful hand motions. She then smiled thoughtfully before making a complete turn like a professional fashion model on a glitzy runway in Paris or New York City.

"No, I'm not too old for you," Montrose finally uttered in his defense, "You're too young for me."

She held the smile as if posing for a photographer. Compassion and bold innocence defined the serious expression on her face. "We'll see, won't we?"

She mounted her bike, and this time she placed her

right foot on the right pedal, smiling bashfully.

"Would you like to see me again?" She pressed the bike's pedal as if to push off. "Better still, would you like to spend some time with me?"

Montrose laughed quietly in an unassuming way. "Why?" He cleared his throat. "Why do you want to spend time with me?"

"Why, why not? What's wrong with you?" Her voice changed from a melodic alto to a much deeper tone. She got off the bike with a sense of urgency and stood very close to Montrose. When their eyes met, they quickly turned away from each other, but in the same direction. As if their fingers had a mind of their own, their hands were cozily joined together. Fingers on opposite hands were interlocked tenderly, lovingly, caringly…

"What's wrong with me…? I'm old; you're young. That's what's wrong with me!"

Her facial expression changed from a strained smile to a curious frown. "So, what! I want to be with you, and you with me, right?"

She paused, and he nodded in an iffy way. "But if we ask too many questions, we'll end up with too many unanswerable or unanswered questions!"

Montrose became increasingly fidgety. After slowly rocking back and forth in the same place, he stopped, steadied himself, stood erect like a soldier in formation, and forced a smile from a puzzled look that formed a confused expression on his face. "I, I don't know. It'd be hard for me to spend time with you..."

"Why?" Her question was a polite demand.

"Most of the time, I don't want to be with me." He paused abruptly as if to avoid a collision with the thoughts that were closing in on him. "But I'm stuck with me."

She smiled. The expression on her face was pleasant, yet serious. "That's the problem. You're spending too much time with yourself. You need to share yourself with me." She held her hands outstretched in front of her as if to balance the scales of reason.

"Let's not measure life by how long we live, but by how much we live. I'd rather spend the rest of our time together than live the rest of my life without you."

Tears once again, though unseen by Jessica, formed in the corners of his eyes. He pretended to wipe sweat from his face to draw attention away from his teary eyes. "You might be right," he said quietly.

"I'm right for sure! You can dream dreams, or you can live life like a dream."

Montrose was once again at a loss for words. While thinking about what to think, or what to say or not say, she added, "I'll see you tomorrow."

"Where and what time," he asked. His voice was filled with hope and doubt.

"Who knows? It may be here in the park or someplace else, but we'll find each other. We always have. I'll see you tomorrow!" She said tomorrow as if it were a fated fact.

She walked slowly to the bike with a graceful stride. Getting back on the bike was as spellbinding as when she got off it. She stood up on the right pedal and pushed off.

Rufus Rawls

7 Dream Catcher

The sun ducked slowly behind the tree line. Jessica disappeared around the curve blanketed with a row of thick pine trees. Montrose looked searchingly in that direction, straining his eyes, hoping to get a departing glimpse of her. Unexpected silhouette images of Jessica appeared and disappeared among the gaps in the tree line.

Montrose considered himself a sensible person, but he was confused and unsure of what to make of Jessica. An old wives' tale, or whatever it was, flooded his mind: "You can't believe nothing you hear and only half of what you see." Whoever came up with that saying wasn't thinking about Montrose, but he believed it was a perfect fit for his situation.

Anyway, there was one thing he did know for sure: With Jessica, he had seen, heard, and experienced, in a short time, a lifetime of joy that he didn't want to end. With his emotions running in overdrive, his mind hopscotched from reasonable to ridiculous conclusions and unanswered questions: Was the death of Dream the birth of Jessica? If she is, what should I do?

He stopped and did the math: Her thirty-first

birthday would seem, at least to Montrose, less life-changing than his fiftieth would to him. And when she turns fifty, Montrose would be sixty-nine. Despite how he felt, he couldn't resist thinking of Jessica as a wife, not a caregiver. The fact that he even thought of her becoming his wife scared him to the point that he tried to stop thinking what he was thinking, and feeling what he was feeling.

As he struggled to think things through, the crazier and more confusing were his thoughts. He did admit to himself that in nineteen years, he would be sixty-eight years old, whether he was with Jessica or not. So, he decided if blessed with the chance to be with her, he would gladly jump off the proverbial bridge of love to live his romantic pipedreams that could be fulfilled if he built a safety net to guard and protect their love down the bumpy pathway of the unknowns.

As Montrose replayed the recent events in his mind, he didn't want his encounter with Jessica to end, so he continued to look in the direction she was last seen. If squinting and straining his eyes had allowed him to see her beyond the tree line, he definitely would have seen her riding off into the sunset. Even though she was now clearly out of sight and his inability to see her was proof she was out of sight, he continued to look for her anyway. Desperately wanting to spend just a little more precious time with her, though she had been gone only five minutes, did not stop him from searching for her. If given another chance, he would tell Jessica all the sweet things he wanted to tell her when they were together.

He unwillingly accepted the fact she was no longer in the park, but that didn't stop him from wanting to see her. Still looking, squinting, and straining his eyes, he decided to look forward to seeing her tomorrow, though it seemed a lifetime away. In a final attempt to see Jessica, Montrose looked beyond the tree line once more, hoping to get a glimpse of her among the distant trees, but saw several joggers resting near a water fountain. When he refocused the second time, he didn't see Jessica, but what he saw was much more life-changing than seeing her. A vision appeared in an image resembling a large television screen. Or maybe it was a hologram image or something. Whatever it was, it was floating in midair directly in front of Montrose.

What he saw and heard were both exciting and unbelievable, though he believed it anyway. The railroad crossing where he last saw Dream, though miles away, appeared before his astonished eyes. He not only saw Dream, but he also heard and saw the train. Most alarming of all, he saw the gunman in the red Plymouth. Unlike the last dream that ended with Dream being murdered, in this open vision she made it across the tracks before the gunman could shoot her. Once the vision of the train disappeared, Montrose saw a police officer handcuffing the gunman, but Dream was nowhere to be seen. He was overjoyed that she had prayerfully escaped to safety, though he was equally concerned that she was clearly out of sight.

Montrose's concerns and joy were now running neck and neck. With his mind now marooned on an island of unchartered possibilities, he searched for a way back to the shores of reality. Although shipwrecked, confused, and unsure of what to think or do, he knew Dream was much more than a dream. She was a true-to-life woman who had come to him in the person of Jessica. No longer obsessed with trying to figure out how these mysterious events were possible; he knew Dream and Jessica were the same woman. With that knowledge, he leaped and jumped onto a shabby bench that barely supported the sudden jolt of his weight. Standing on his tiptoes, he screamed, shattering the silence that filled the park. His voice echoed off the walls of the sky and caused two robins perching in a nearby pecan tree to take flight. He then jumped off the bench, landed on his left foot, and with a big smile on his face, he knew without a doubt that some dreams do indeed come true.

He was now in a hurry to go home and go to bed before his normal bedtime, not to dream for the sake of dreaming, but to dream about tomorrow when he and

Jessica would get together for the last time. It would prayerfully be the last time because he would never again allow anything or anyone to separate them, although he didn't know exactly what he needed to do to make that happen. Not only that, the thought of a lasting relationship was an exciting but scary thing to even think about. He did know what to do, though unsure he would do it. So, he decided to look forward to tomorrow, when he would say hello to Jessica and goodbye to his past, filled with pain and unfulfilled longings.

With shallow breathing and a rapid heartbeat, he managed to regain his mental composure and physical balance. He walked slowly toward the street with a renewed sense of purpose. His body was now relaxed and calmer, but the thought of not knowing where he would see Jessica tomorrow confused his thinking. He was unsure whether to think or not about the endless possibilities unfolding in real time that had been a recurring dream but were now much more! Not knowing the unknown did not stop him from looking forward to getting to know the woman of his dreams. While trying to convince himself that he wasn't too old for Jessica, he was unable to ignore the fact that she might be too young for him. When he remembered hearing, someone say, "Age is nothing but a number," he prayed his number was an unimportant number to Jessica.

He quickly looked over his left shoulder. The two robins had returned to the pecan tree and perched beside each other on a rotten limb. He wondered whether the dead limb was a good or bad omen or no sign at all. Either way, his heart smiled as he walked away. Without necessarily intending to, Montrose looked heavenward for an answer to his longings for a life of love and happiness with Jessica, who is Dream Love, who wasn't a dream after all. But plain old commonsense weighed the odds and warned Montrose that expecting his dream to be fulfilled was not only unlikely, but too unbelievable to believe.

When he thought seriously about their age difference, his hope dropped quickly from the lofty clouds of a stormy pipedream. The thunderous thoughts, looming with uneasiness and flashes of uncertainty, formed, and disappeared on the horizon of his mind, and an overcast of fear attacked his troubled heart. He felt like a ton of wet bricks had fallen on his head. He understood they would grow older each day, but he also understood a day older for her would be less of a day older than it would be for him. Since he began his journey in life before Jessica, his would likely end sooner than hers. Not only that, but he was concerned that time and his age might prevent him from fulfilling her needs when she needed them and him the most.

Montrose was unwilling to give in to the fears that he was overwhelmed by. He was hoping against hope that life would somehow reverse the tides of time, that God would bless him, delay the effects of the aging process, at least for a little while, and allow Jessica and him to live their dream lives together. As incredible as his dream was, he knew it wasn't a twisted nightmare.

He stopped for a moment to reflect on everything that had happened before continuing to walk toward the street that was bustling with activity.

Traffic and people were going and coming, and so was Montrose…

44